To the memory of my lovely Grandad Percy
and Uncle David.

And for my brave, kind and wonderful Dad,
who was and will always be my guiding light xx

A TEMPLAR BOOK

First published in the UK in 2022 by Templar Books,
an imprint of Bonnier Books UK
4th Floor, Victoria House,
Bloomsbury Square, London WC1B 4DA
Owned by Bonnier Books
Sveavägen 56, Stockholm, Sweden
www.bonnierbooks.co.uk

ISBN 978-1-78741-918-6

This book was typeset in Adobe Caslon Pro
The illustrations were created with pencil and ink

The recipe should be followed under adult supervision

Edited by Ruth Symons
Designed by Genevieve Webster
Production by Nick Read

Printed in Lithuania

The BAKER by the SEA

PAULA WHITE

templar
books

If you keep walking over the hills . . .

. . . and across the fields,

. . . you will come to the edge, where the land meets the sea.

And on this edge,
where the beach begins,
lies a village.

This is my home.

Our home, our beach village by the sea.

We have fish merchants,
and smokers that smoke the fish,
blacksmiths and basketmakers,
butchers and bakers.
There are cosy cafés and
tiny shops that sell everything
you might need.

Everyone works hard, by the sea.

The sail-makers make sails and the boatbuilders build
and mend the boats, so the fishermen can go to sea.
The net-makers make nets and the rope-makers make rope,
so the fishermen can catch the fish.
The coopers make the barrels for pickling,
and the Scotch fisher-girls prepare, pack and pickle the fish.

The sea is the beating heart of all we do.

As the sun sets slowly behind the cliff, the weary workers
make their way home and the village begins to rest.

And at night, while the fishermen are fishing, the village
lies sleeping, gently soothed by the rhythm of the sea.

In the quiet, I think of the hard-working people,
still outside in the cold and rain.

When I am older, I am going to be a fisherman.
I will brave the waves and windy weather,
and catch the finest and freshest fish,
for the people of the village by the sea.

On the boat, we will work together,
handling, hoisting and heaving the ropes,
ready for our biggest catch.

When the wind begins to whistle, the sky turns inky black
and waves as tall as houses come crashing down, we will know what to do,
for we bold fishermen can battle any storm.

And when we head for home, as the sea starts to calm and
a heavy blanket of fog rolls in, we will search for the bright, white light,
high on the cliff, and listen for the bellow of the foghorn.

We will steer safely home, home to our village,
where the land meets the sea.

My father is not a fisherman.

He is the baker, and every day, before the sun rises,
and before the boats come in, he is safe and warm inside,
busily baking. And a comforting waft of fresh bread
welcomes a new day.

He bakes bread,

buns,

and biscuits.

He bakes baskets of bread for Babs' Corner Café,

where Babs makes the best bacon butties, the boatbuilders' favourite.

He delivers bags of piping hot buns
for the tough Scotch fisher-girls.

And he sells boxes of biscuits

for the brave fishermen to take to sea.

Sometimes I help my father, and as the glow from the oven
keeps us toasty and warm, I think of all the people, working outside
in the wet and windy weather.

I wonder, if my father could make a barrel or build a big boat,
why is he just a baker?

And I ask him,
"Have you ever been to sea?"

"Yes," he replies. "When I was a boy.
I tried it once and even twice and
I knew it wasn't for me."

He pats his apron,
and a floury cloud fills the air.
I see his pride shine through.

"I became a baker, son,
it's what I wanted to do."

"Just imagine if there were no bread, buns and biscuits?

If Babs at the Corner Café served breadless bacon butties,
what would the boatbuilders do?

And if the Scotch fisher-girls, out in the open in the bitter cold,
didn't get their piping hot buns to warm their nimble fingers . . .
then how would they pack the fish?

The fish would pile up, with no room for more."

"And what would happen to the fishermen who fished until dawn, without their biscuits dipped in hot broth and dunked in their tea?

They would be too cold and hungry to catch the fish,
out in the dangerous sea."

But thanks to the baker, everyone has had their fill today, their bellies warm inside.
And with the boats safely home, the harbour comes to life,
busy and bustling with lifting and lugging, unloading the precious catch.

As the morning sun climbs higher in the sky,
a tired fisherman stops by.
He looks to my father and they share weary smiles.

Then, without a word,
he passes my father the finest and fattest fish,
with a thankful glint in his eye.

I look at my father and feel proud.

For without the bread, buns and biscuits,
that he busily bakes before the sun rises,
the people of the village could not
go on as they do.

When I am older, I am going to be a baker,
just like my father, in the village by the sea.

For everyone works hard here.

Everyone, including me.

ICING
SUGAR

Hot Coconut Buns

Ingredients

225g self-raising flour

½ tsp baking powder

125g unsalted butter, cut into cubes

125g caster sugar

50g desiccated coconut

85g dried mixed fruit of your choice

1 egg, beaten

1–3 tbsp milk

A few drops of vanilla essence

Whole glacé cherries for the top

Granulated sugar for sprinkling (optional)

Method

1. Sift the flour and baking powder into a large bowl.
2. Add the butter and lightly rub together with your fingertips until the mixture resembles fine breadcrumbs.
3. Stir in the caster sugar, coconut and dried fruit and mix well.
4. Make a well in the centre of the mixture; add the beaten egg, 1 tbsp of the milk and a few drops of vanilla essence and mix well to create a fairly stiff dough mixture. If the mixture is still dry, add milk, 1 tbsp at a time until the dough holds together.
5. Lightly grease two baking trays or line with parchment paper.
6. Place dessert spoonfuls of the mixture on the baking trays allowing space for the mixture to spread.
7. Top the buns with a glacé cherry in the centre (or more if you want!) and sprinkle with granulated sugar, if using.
8. Bake in a pre-heated oven at 200°C (Fan 180°C/400°F/Gas Mark 6) for 15 minutes or until golden brown and firm to touch.

This recipe is taken from my grandad's notebook. The quantities have been scaled down so you can bake them for your family or friends – assuming you don't run a bakery! They're the same taste the fisher-girls would have enjoyed at 11 o'clock every morning.

Enjoy!

Paula

The beach village of this tale was once situated
in Paula's hometown on the East Coast of Suffolk in England.
For over 100 years, it was home to a thriving fishing community.
Paula's grandad Percy was a baker for the village
but sometimes felt guilty for not being a fisherman.

This story is for him.

The Baker by the Sea was the overall winner of the 2019 Templar Illustration Award